Story / Cuento
Alma Flor Ada

Illustrations / Ilustraciones
Angela Domínguez

CHILDREN'S BOOK PRESS SAN FRANCISCO, CALIFORNIA

Introduction

Celebrations are part of every culture. Families celebrate birthdays and weddings, and society celebrates historical dates and accomplished people. Latinos love to celebrate, to eat with family and friends, to play music, to dance, to share joy. Any occasion is good for a *fiesta*.

The city of San Antonio, Texas, especially loves *fiestas*. Twice a year, during Fiesta Week in April and again right before the Christmas holidays, the city puts on extravagant river parades of beautifully decorated barges. On Cinco de Mayo, huge crowds come to Market Square to eat delicious food, listen to *mariachi* bands, and enjoy traditional arts and crafts from different parts of Mexico. There isn't an official river parade, but some families rent barges and cruise down the river while listening to the lively music that envelopes the city.

Some *fiestas* develop greater meaning over time. For example, Cinco de Mayo commemorates the Battle of Puebla, when on May 5, 1861, the Mexican army defeated the French, who had invaded Mexico. Today, in the United States, Cinco de Mayo celebrates the contributions of all Latinos to life in our society.

— **Alma Flor Ada**

Introducción

Las celebraciones son parte integral de toda cultura. Las familias celebran nacimientos y bodas, y la sociedad celebra fechas históricas y los aniversarios de personas reconocidas. A los latinos nos encanta celebrar, comer con la familia y los amigos, tocar música, bailar, compartir la alegría. Cualquier ocasión merece una fiesta.

A la ciudad de San Antonio, Texas, le encantan las fiestas. Dos veces al año, en abril durante la Semana de Fiestas e inmediatamente antes de las Navidades, la ciudad organiza grandes espectáculos por el río, con balsas maravillosamente decoradas. Durante el Cinco de Mayo, miles de personas se reúnen en Market Square para comer platillos deliciosos, oír música de mariachi, y mirar y comprar artesanías traídas de distintas partes de México. Aunque no hay un desfile oficial por el río, es común que las familias renten balsas para bajar por el río y disfrutar de la alegre música que envuelve la ciudad.

Algunas fiestas cobran mayor importancia al pasar el tiempo. Por ejemplo, el Cinco de Mayo conmemora la Batalla de Puebla de 1861, en la que el ejército mexicano derrotó a los franceses que habían invadido México. Hoy, en los Estados Unidos, el Cinco de Mayo celebra las contribuciones de los latinos y latinas a la sociedad.

— **Alma Flor Ada**

Everyone was very busy, running and rushing, preparing for the Cinco de Mayo celebration. The children were particularly excited. The family had rented a barge and they were planning to have a picnic on the San Antonio River.

Wonderful smells came from the kitchen. Music filled the house, inviting feet to tap to its rhythm, and bright paper flowers and shiny ribbons were scattered everywhere. So it was not surprising that Elena forgot to close Perico's cage door after she fed him.

Todos estaban muy ocupados. Corrían apresurados preparándose para la celebración del Cinco de Mayo. Los niños eran los más entusiasmados. Su familia había alquilado una balsa e iban a tener un picnic en el río San Antonio.

De la cocina salían olores deliciosos. La música llenaba la casa, invitando a los pies a moverse a su ritmo, y por todas partes había flores de papel y cintas de colores brillantes. Por eso no era de extrañar que a Elena se le olvidara cerrar la jaula de Perico después de darle de comer.

"Look, Mami, Perico wants to be part of Cinco de Mayo, too," said Martita when she saw the parrot flapping about in the kitchen.

Perico was indeed fascinated by all of the movement in the kitchen. Making *tamales* seemed to be something he could take part in. He loved *tamales.* Surely he could help make them!

—Mira, Mami, Perico también quiere celebrar el Cinco de Mayo —dijo Martita cuando vio al loro batir sus alas en la cocina.

Perico estaba realmente fascinado por todo lo que pasaba en la cocina. Le pareció que podía ayudar a hacer tamales. A él le encantaban los tamales, así que ¡seguramente podría ayudar a prepararlos!

"Let me help! Let me help!" Perico cried. It was a sentence he had learned recently: little Martita was always asking to be allowed to help.

But Abuela and Tía Lupe didn't think that Perico could help.

"Perico, go away! Let us work!," they cried, moving their arms wildly to shoo him away.

—¡Quiero ayudar! ¡Quiero ayudar! —exclamó Perico. Era una frase que había aprendido hacía muy poco. Martita siempre estaba pidiendo que la dejaran ayudar.

Pero la abuela y Tía Lupe no creían que Perico podía ayudar.

—¡Vete, Perico! ¡Déjanos trabajar! —gritaron, moviendo los brazos para espantarlo.

Elena and her mother were in the living room making flowers with multicolored tissue paper. The festive flowers reminded Perico of the bright colors of the rainforest. He should certainly be able to help make the colorful flowers.

Elena y su madre estaban en la sala haciendo flores de papel de muchos colores. Las bonitas flores hicieron recordar a Perico los colores brillantes de la selva. Seguramente podría ayudar a hacer las flores de colores.

"Let me help! Let me help!" Perico cried.

But Mamá and Elena did not agree.

"Perico, go away! Let us work!" they said and pushed him away.

—¡Quiero ayudar! ¡Quiero ayudar! —exclamó Perico.

Pero Elena y su mamá no estaban de acuerdo.

—¡Vete, Perico! ¡Déjanos trabajar! —le dijeron y lo ahuyentaron para que se fuera.

Lupita and Carmen were in their room dressing up for their *folklórico* dance performance. The bright ribbons that Tía Alicia was braiding into the girls' hair reminded Perico of jungle butterflies fluttering about like winged flowers. Surely Perico could help them get ready.

Lupita y Carmen estaban en su cuarto arreglándose para el baile folklórico. Las cintas brillantes que tía Alicia trenzaba en el pelo de las niñas le recordaron a Perico las mariposas que revoloteaban como flores aladas en la selva. Seguramente él podría ayudarlas a alistarse.

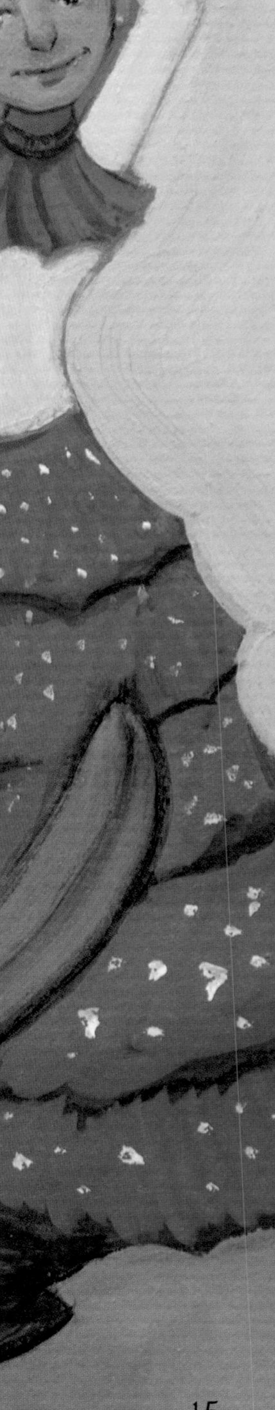

"Let me help! Let me help!" Perico cried, but Tía Alicia wanted to concentrate on what she was doing.

"Perico, go away! Let me work!" she shouted at him.

—¡Quiero ayudar! ¡Quiero ayudar! —exclamó Perico, pero tía Alicia quería concentrarse en lo que estaba haciendo.

—¡Vete, Perico! ¡Déjame trabajar! —le gritó.

Antonio and Francisco were on the front porch practicing their trumpets for their *mariachi* number. The sound reminded Perico of the cries of toucans. Surely he could help them practice.

"Let me help! Let me help!" he cried.

But Antonio and Francisco didn't want any noise while they were practicing.

"Perico, go away! Let us practice!" they replied impatiently.

Antonio y Francisco estaban en la veranda practicando en sus trompetas la pieza de música mariachi que tocarían. El sonido le recordó a Perico los gritos de los tucanes. Seguramente podría ayudarlos a practicar.

—¡Quiero ayudar! ¡Quiero ayudar! —exclamó Perico.

Pero Antonio y Francisco no querían ruido alguno mientras practicaban.

—¡Vete, Perico! ¡Déjanos trabajar! —le contestaron impacientes.

Perico flew off the porch and down the street. What a wonderful smell was coming from the bakery! Don Martín was baking batches upon batches of *pan dulce.*

"Let me help! Let me help!" Perico cried.

"Go away! Go away!" cried Don Martín, very upset. He did not want a parrot in his busy bakery, nor feathers on his *pan dulce.*

Perico se fue volando por la calle. ¡Qué olor delicioso salía de la panadería! Don Martín sacaba hornadas tras hornadas de pan dulce.

—¡Quiero ayudar! ¡Quiero ayudar! —exclamó Perico.

—¡Vete! ¡Vete! —gritó don Martín. No quería tener un perico en su panadería ni plumas en el pan dulce.

¡Sabroso!

Perico flew over the city. Everywhere he looked, people were celebrating. Along the river, people floated by on beautifully decorated barges. It was as if all the flowers of the jungle were floating down the river. Fascinated, Perico decided to perch on a bridge and watch.

Perico voló sobre la ciudad. Había celebraciones por todas partes. La gente se deslizaba sobre el río en balsas hermosamente decoradas. Era como si todas las flores de la selva estuvieran flotando en el río. Fascinado, Perico decidió posarse sobre un puente a mirar.

FELI

Just then Perico saw his family's barge moving gracefully down the river. It was larger and taller than any other barge. But its topmost decoration was too high to pass underneath the bridge. It hit the arch and fell down into the water.

"Oh! What a shame! Our beautiful barge!" Perico's family cried.

Perico looked at the barge. This was his chance to help!

Justo entonces vio la balsa de su familia acercarse lentamente por el río. Era más grande y alta que las demás. Pero como el adorno en la parte superior era demasiado alto para pasar bajo el puente, chocó contra el arco y cayó al agua.

—¡Ay, qué pena! ¡Nuestra hermosa balsa! —dijo afligida la familia de Perico.

Perico miró a la balsa. ¡Por fin podría ayudar!

Perico flew down and perched on top of the flowers that crowned the gaily decorated barge. He looked quite perfect there.

Perico voló hacia la balsa y se posó sobre las flores que coronaban su alegre decoración. Se veía realmente perfecto.

Martita cried, "Mamá! Look! Perico found a way to help!"

Mamá and Abuela, Antonio and Francisco, Lupe and Carmen, and Tía Lupe and Tía Alicia all looked up.

"Hooray! *Bravo!*" they cheered.

Martita levantó la vista y exclamó: —¡Mamá! ¡Mira! ¡Perico encontró el modo de ayudar!

Al oír a Martita, todos miraron hacia arriba... su mamá y su abuela, Antonio y Francisco, Lupe y Carmen, y tía Lupe y tía Alicia.

Todos gritaron alegremente: —¡Bravo! *¡Hooray!*

Perico just nodded, swaying to the music of the *mariachi* band as the barge sailed slowly and gracefully by. He had finally found the perfect way to help. It wasn't by trying to do what others could do, but by doing what no one else could. And he did it by being himself, his wonderful self.

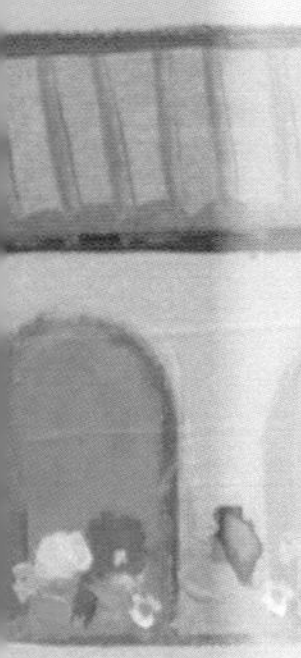

Perico saludó con la cabeza, meciéndose al compás de la música de los mariachis mientras la balsa seguía bajando lentamente por el río. Había encontrado el mejor modo de ayudar. No era imitar lo que otros hacían, sino hacer aquello que nadie más podía hacer. Y lo hizo simplemente siendo él mismo.

ALMA FLOR ADA is an award-winning children's book author, a gifted translator, and one of the leaders in the field of bilingual education in the United States. Born in Cuba, Alma Flor received her PhD at the Pontifical Catholic University of Lima, Perú, did her post-doctoral research at Harvard University as a Fellow of the Radcliffe Institute, and is a Fulbright Research Scholar. A Professor Emerita at the University of San Francisco, Alma Flor currently lives in Northern California's Marin County.

For Elva Fellers and her cousins. May you always find joy in helping. With much love from your great-aunt, —AFA

ANGELA DOMÍNGUEZ was born in Mexico City and raised in Texas. Growing up, she loved to read and to draw. Angela holds an MFA in Illustration from the Academy of Art in San Francisco. When not drawing, she enjoys being outdoors and drinking strong coffee. She hopes that her illustrations make people of all ages smile. Angela currently lives in Fresno, California.

Photo of Angela by ValJean Anderson.

To my family and friends. Thank you for all your support, confidence, and help. I can't thank y'all enough. —AD

Library of Congress Cataloging-in-Publication Data
Ada, Alma Flor.
Let me help! / story, Alma Flor Ada ; illustrations, Angela Domínguez = ¡Quiero ayudar! / cuento, Alma Flor Ada ; illustraciones, Angela Domínguez.
p. cm.
Summary: A pet parrot tries to help his human family prepare for the Cinco de Mayo festivities in San Antonio, Texas.
ISBN-13: 978-0-89239-232-2 (hardcover)
[1. Cinco de Mayo (Mexican holiday)—Fiction. 2. Parrots—Fiction. 3. Helpfulness—Fiction. 4. Hispanic Americans—Fiction. 5. San Antonio (Tex.)—Fiction. 6. Spanish language materials—Bilingual.] I. Domínguez, Angela N., ill. II. Title. III. Title: ¡Quiero ayudar!
PZ73.A245 2010
[E]—dc22 2009028501

Publisher/Executive Director: Lorraine García-Nakata
Executive Editor: Dana Goldberg
Art Direction & Design: Carl Angel
Thanks to Rosalyn Sheff, Citlali Martínez, Teresa Mlawer, and the staff of Children's Book Press: Janet, Rod, and Imelda.

This book was printed in Hong Kong by First Choice Printing Co. Ltd via Marwin Productions in October 2009, and meets or exceeds required safety standards and regulations.
10 9 8 7 6 5 4 3 2 1

Children's Book Press is a 501(c)3 nonprofit organization. Our work is made possible in part by the following contributors: The WalMart Foundation/California Advisory Council, National Endowment for the Arts, AT&T Foundation, San Francisco Foundation, San Francisco Arts Commission, Wells Fargo/Wachovia Foundation, Stephen Santos Rico, Carlota del Portillo, Union Bank of California, Children's Book Press Board of Directors, Anonymous Fund of the Greater Houston Community Foundation, Herbert and Nylda Gemple, Rose Gilbault, and many others.

Distributed to the book trade by Publishers Group West. Quantity discounts available for nonprofit use. Visit us on the web at:
www.childrensbookpress.org